Printed in Malaysia • First Edition • 1 3 5 7 9 10 8 6 4 2 • H106-9333-5-13333
Designed by Whitney Manger
Text is set in Telegraph.
Art created in pen and ink on Arches paper with digital coloring.

Library of Congress Cataloging-in-Publication Data

Ruzzier, Sergio.
    Bear and Bee : too busy / by Sergio Ruzzier.—1st ed.
      p. cm.
    Summary: Bear wants to have fun with his friend Bee, but Bee is too busy.
    ISBN 978-1-4231-5961-2
    [1. Friendship—Fiction. 2. Bears—Fiction. 3. Bees—Fiction.] I. Title.
PZ7.R9475Bft 2014
    [E]—dc23   2012037300

Reinforced binding
Visit www.disneyhyperionbooks.com

To Gloria and Max

BEAR -and- Bee
TOO BUSY

by Sergio Ruzzier

Disney • Hyperion Books
New York

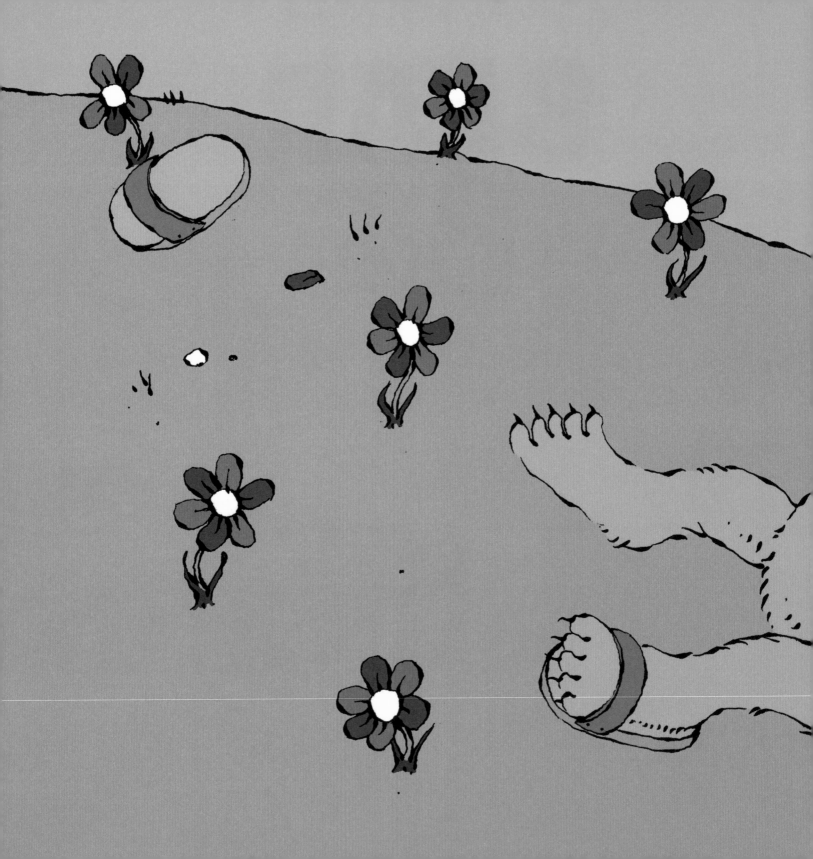

"Wheeeeee!"

"Bee!" calls Bear.
"Come and roll down the hill with me.
You will love it!"

"No, thank you, Bear," says Bee.

"I'm too busy to roll down the hill."

"Hmm. What else is there to do?" says Bear.

"Hooray!"

"Bee!" says Bear.
"Come and climb the tree with me.
You will love it!"

"No, thank you, Bear," says Bee.
"I'm too busy to climb the tree."

"Hmm. What else is there to do?" says Bear.

"Whoopee!"

"Bee!" says Bear.
"Come and splash in the pond with me.
You will love it!"

"No, thank you, Bear," says Bee.
"I'm too busy to splash in the pond."

"Oh, Bee," says Bear.
"Having fun is not as fun without you."

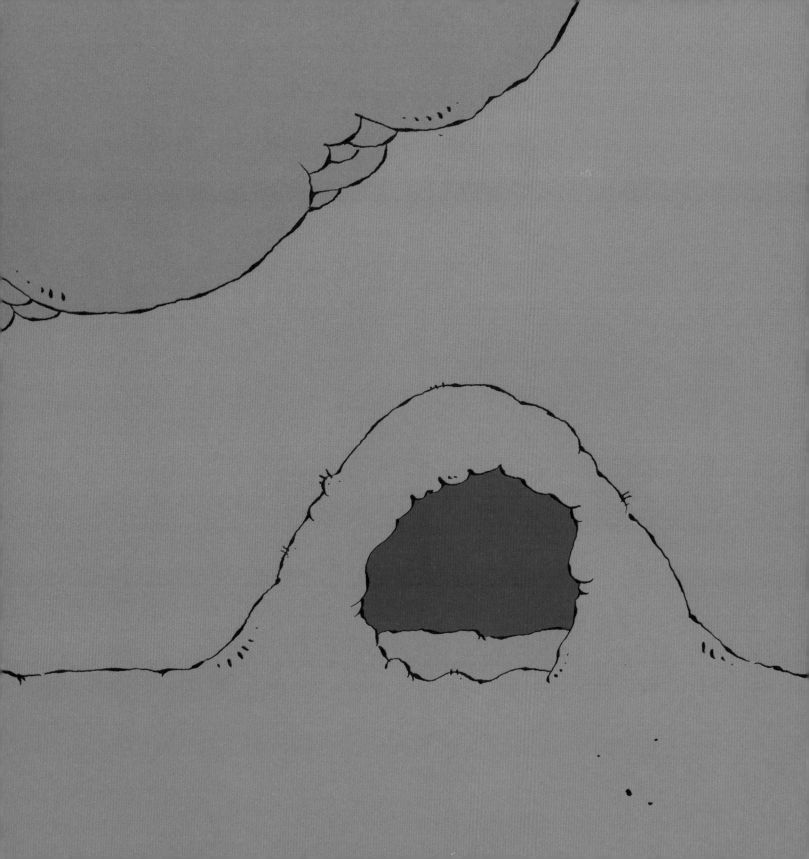

"Oh!" says Bee.
"The moon is out!"

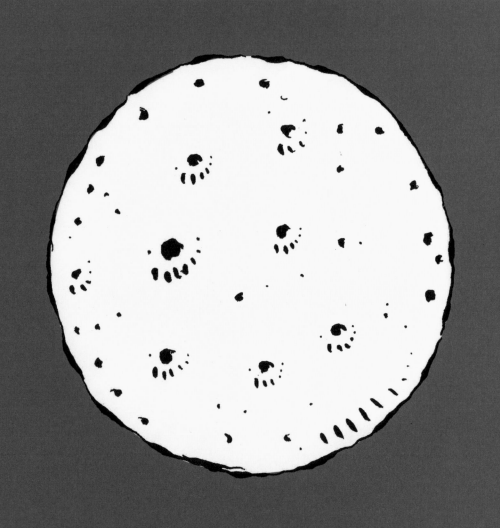

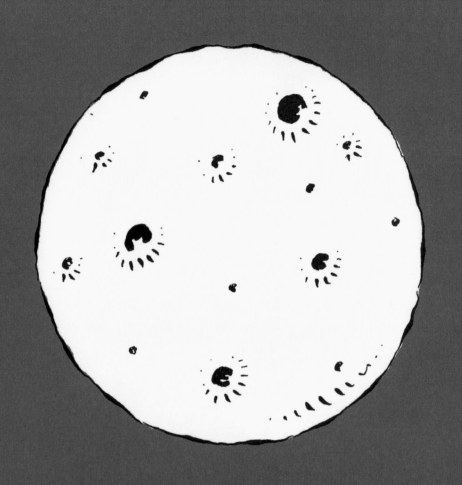

"Bear!" says Bee.
"Come and look at the moon with me.
You will love it!"

"No, thank you, Bee," says Bear.

"I'm too busy sleeping to look at the moon."

"But, Bear, the moon is not
as lovely without you," says Bee.

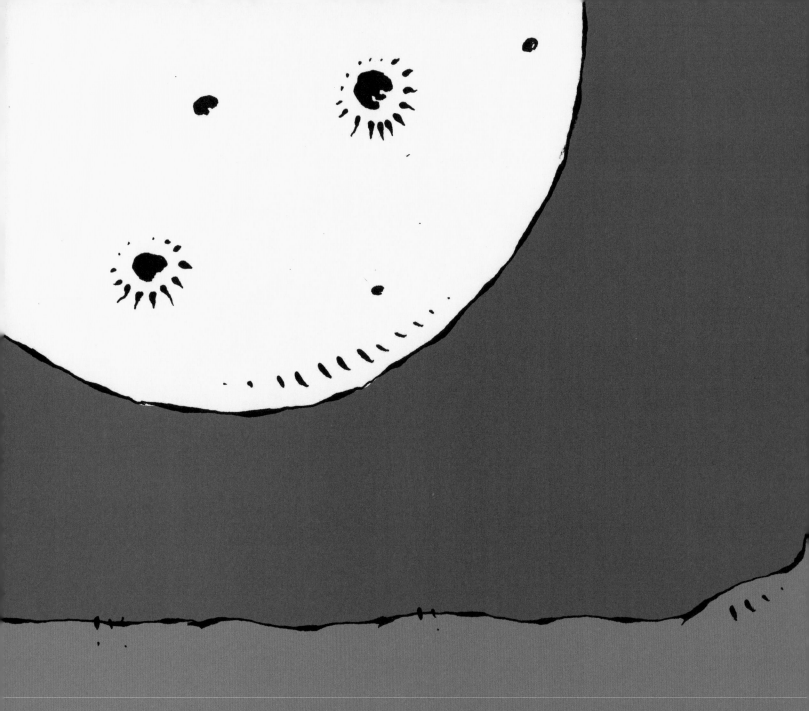

"What can we do that both of us will love?"

"I know what!"

"There's nothing as lovely
as spending time with you, Bear."

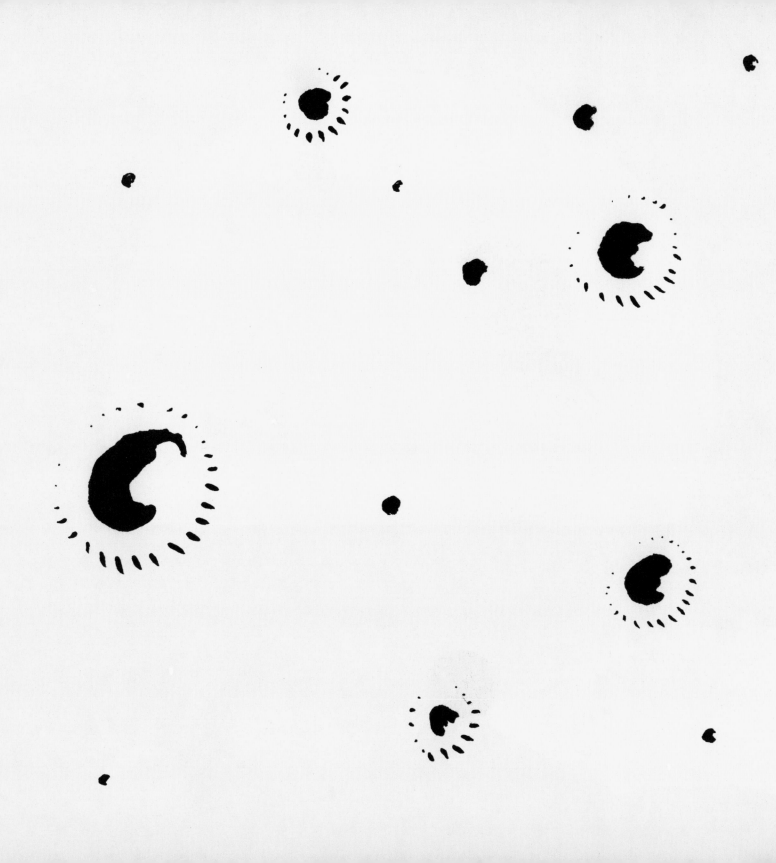